FIRST EDITION
Jake the Snake, Professor Hooper Place, LTD

ISBN 1-889803-00-6

Published by: Professor Hooper Place, LTD
                  2 Cox Avenue
                  Harvey Cedars, NJ 08008
                  (800) 6 HOOPER (800) 646-6737

Printed in United States of America
By: H & W Communications Network, Inc.
                  2649 Gardner Road
                  Broadview, IL 60153
                  (708)865-7422

Manufactured in the United States of America

Jake the Snake went out for a walk
    and slid in his usual way.
He slithered along the sunny path;
    it was such a beautiful day.

He greeted his friends in the garden;
    they were used to seeing him there.
The bugs and bees, the ants and flies,
    and his friend, the old grey hare.

"Good morning Jake," they said to him,
    "It's such a gorgeous day."
"Yesssssssssss it is," Jake replied
    in his usual snaky way.

Through the garden, across the walk
    to the lawn and when he'd done,
he stretched out on a great big rock
    and laid out in the sun.

The sun was warm and made him tired
    and soon Jake fell asleep.
He snored a gentle hissssssing sound
    but not another peep.

Suddenly he was wakened
    by an unfamiliar sound-
it was a woman screaming
    and jumping up and down!

As he looked up at the woman
    who yelled and screamed at Jake,
he thought, "You're so much bigger than I,
    why yell at a little snake?"

But he saw there was no reasoning
    as she continued to rant and rave,
so Jake sought out the security
    of a bush whose name was Dave.

Thought Jake, "She must be scared of me;
    that's the trouble here.
I think if she got to know me,
    she wouldn't have this fear.

How can I get to know her?
    How can I make her my friend?
I think if I go and just say hi,
    the screaming will never end!"

"Maybe she would like me
    if I helped her with her work.
She'd see that I was friendly;
    she wouldn't go berserk."

He looked around the big backyard
    to see what he could do.
He saw an opportunity when
    the clothesline broke in two.

Jake went over and grabbed the
    line with his mouth and tail.
Then he pulled the clothesline
    tight and held it like a rail.

Soon, the woman brought out her clothes;
  she didn't make a sound.
She went to hang them on the line;
  her eyes looked to the ground.

Because she wasn't watching when she
  went to hang the clothes,
she took a big wood clothespin
  and stuck it on Jake's nose!

"That hurt a bit," thought Jake the Snake,
  "of that there's little doubt.
Perhaps I'm having second thoughts
  'bout trying to help out."

Nonetheless, poor Jake held on
　　until the clothes were dry.
The woman came and got the clothes
　　and Jake just said "Oh my!"

"I'd hate to go through that again,
　　that's very plain to see.
I think I need a better way,
　　to meet this family."

Jake slid down the clothes pole.
　　He looked and noted that
some children were out riding bikes,
　　but one bike had a flat.

When Jake saw this dilemma,
    he thought, "I truly feel
I can help that poor boy out,
    by becoming a bike-snake-wheel!"

He crawled across the driveway
    and up onto the bike.
He stretched himself out on the rim
    'til the tire and he were alike.

Soon the boy jumped on the bike and
    rode 'round for a while.
Jake got dizzy as he spun around;
    the kid could only smile.

"Thank you much," he said to Jake,
    "that was kind of you.
I had no idea of all the
    things a snake could do!"

"Yesssssssss," said Jake, who wobbled 'round,
 "I'm glad you liked it, son.
With kids, a snake, and some ideas,
 we can have great fun!"

They went to the baseball diamond
 where Jake discovered that
by tensing all his muscles
 he could be a baseball bat!

And when the baseball players
 started getting bored,
Jake, the makeshift baseball bat,
 turned into a sword.

That was fun, but soon got old;
　　they wanted something new.
So Jake, the kid's new playmate,
　　he showed them what to do.

A hockey stick, a vaulting bar,
　　a runner for their sled;
a coiled spring, a hula hoop.
　　"We love you Jake," they said.

"I love you too," Jake replied,
    "but I should be getting back."
"Before you leave," the children
    said, "come over for a snack."

So Jake went over to the house
for a sandwich and a pear.
He only hoped their mom stayed out
and didn't see him there.

But Mom came in the kitchen
   saw Jake and yelled, "Get lost!"
Said Jake the Snake to his new friends,
   "I think I'm getting tossed!"

The kids said, "Mom, that's not fair,
   to send away our friend.
Just because he is a snake,
   our friendship should not end!"

"Jake's been very kind to us.
    He played with us all day.
He has taught us many games;
    besides, you always say:

We should judge a person
    by what's inside, not what's out.
And Jake's been very good to us;
    of that, there is no doubt!

So c'mon Mom, please don't think
    of him as just a snake.
He has been a friend to us!"
    Mom thought and looked at Jake.

"I guess I shouldn't be so quick
    to judge those I don't know.
I'm sorry, Jake," the mother said.
    "Please stay. Please do not go.

A lesson has been learned here,
    and it was learned by me.
Never judge a man (or snake)
    by what you simply see.

Rather, get to know him,
    and see what you can find.
You might find that people
    are truly good and kind."

And if you try this everyday,
    what you'll find; who knows?
Maybe it will be a snake
    who helps you hang your
clothes!